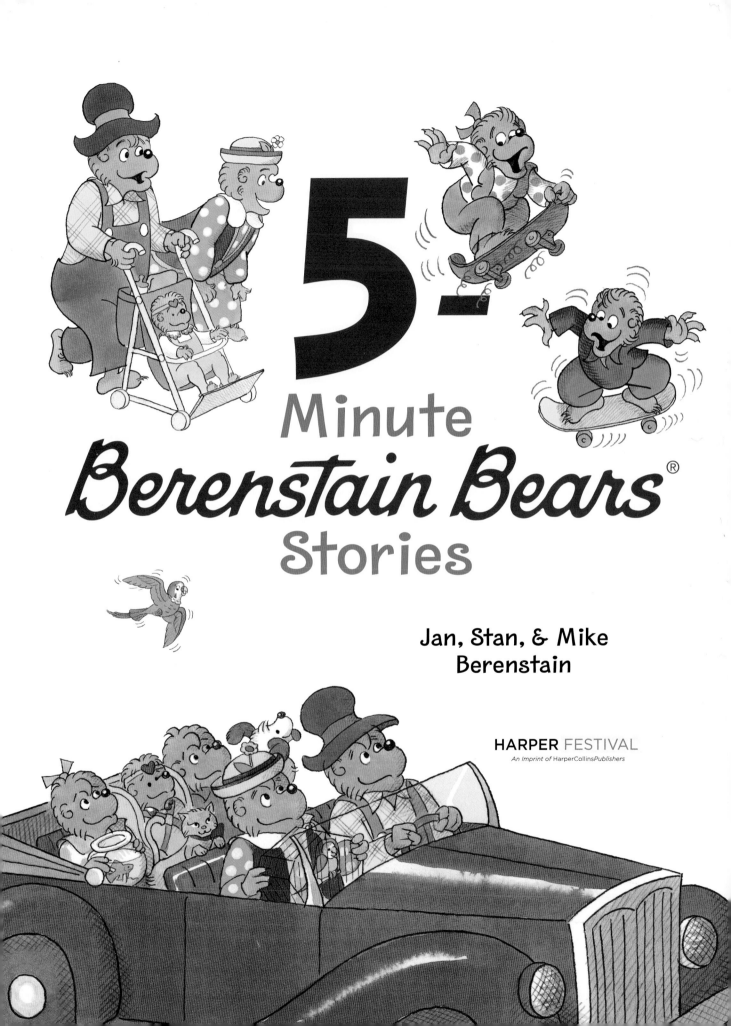

5-Minute
Minute
Berenstain Bears®
Stories

Jan, Stan, & Mike
Berenstain

HARPER FESTIVAL
An Imprint of HarperCollinsPublishers

HarperFestival is an imprint of HarperCollins Publishers.

5-Minute Berenstain Bears Stories
Copyright © 2015 by Berenstain Publishing, Inc.

For information address HarperCollins Children's Books,
a division of HarperCollins Publishers,
195 Broadway, New York, NY 10007.
www.harpercollinschildrens.com

ISBN 978-0-06-236018-2

Typography by Lori S Malkin
16 17 18 19 SCP 10 9 8 7 6 5 4

First edition

CONTENTS

The Berenstain Bears
at the AQUARIUM

On a sunny Saturday afternoon, the Bear family piled into their big red car. Papa Bear told everyone that he was taking them on a surprise trip. The whole family was excited. They soon arrived at their destination.

"Here we are at the aquarium," said Papa Bear, pointing at the entrance sign.

"The what?" asked Sister.

"The ah-KWAR-ee-um," said Mama. "It is a zoo of the sea."

"There are many things to see," Papa said.

"Cool!" said Brother. "I want to see the whale!"

"I want to see the dolphins!" said Sister.

After parking the car, the Bear family entered the aquarium. Papa Bear paid for their tickets, and soon the family was strolling past amazing underwater creatures.

Papa Bear looked at his map of the aquarium. "What shall we see first?" he asked the cubs.

"The whale," said Brother.

"The dolphins," said Sister.

Mama Bear pointed to the tanks in front of them. They were filled with brightly colored fish from all over the world. "First, let's see the fish," she said.

"All right," said the cubs, disappointed.

As the cubs explored the aquarium, they quickly cheered up. They spotted hundreds of fish that they had never seen before.

"This swordfish has a very long nose," said Papa, approaching one of the tanks.

"Pointy, too," added Brother.

"The flounder is very flat," said Mama, looking inside another fish tank.

"His eyes are on the same side," said Sister. "Ugh!"

Papa pointed to a large fish with long whiskers. "Here is a catfish," he said.

"It sure looks like a cat," said Brother.

On the other side of the fish exhibit, Mama found another fish with a funny name. "Here is a dogfish," she told Sister and Honey.

"It does not look like a dog," said Sister, frowning.

Then Brother and Sister spotted a sign for another aquarium exhibit. It was exactly what they both wanted to see.

"This way to the whale!" shouted Brother.

"This way to the dolphins!" yelled Sister.

But before they reached the whale and dolphins, the Bear family passed many more undersea creatures. In one room, they saw an octopus.

"Which end is the front?" asked Mama, studying the creature.

"I'm not sure," replied Papa.

In another room, they saw a jellyfish exhibit. Papa
pointed at one of the strange, balloonlike creatures. "Those
long strings can sting you," Papa told the cubs.

"Not if we stay out of the tank," said Mama.

But the cubs weren't interested. They
wanted to get to the main attractions.

"Where is the whale?" asked Brother.

"And where are the dolphins?"
asked Sister.

"Just hold on," Papa said. "There is
plenty of time to see all the animals."

The next room
didn't have any
fish. It was filled with
black-and-white birds.
The birds slid down an
icy slide and then splashed
beneath the water.

"Look at those penguins
swim!" said Mama, surprised.

"Look at them dive!" said Papa.

"Why don't they fly?" asked Brother.

"Because they can't," said Papa.

"Why don't they walk?" asked Sister.

"Some of them do," said Brother.

Finally, the Bear family reached the end of the indoor exhibits. They headed outside to see the other animals.

"The otters are so cute," said Mama, bending to see the playful animals in their pool.

"It is fun to watch them slide," said Papa.

Then Brother and Sister spotted another sign for their favorite attractions.

"I wish I could see the whale," said Brother.

"I wish I could see the dolphins," said Sister.

The Bear family hurried along to the seal pool. It was feeding time. The seals made a lot of noise! Their trainers gave them fish to eat.

"This makes me so hungry," said Papa.

"Here is a place to eat," said Mama.

The Bears decided to have lunch and watch the seals.

After lunch, the cubs spotted another sign. It read,
WHALE & DOLPHIN SHOW TODAY!
"Hooray! The whale, at last!" said Brother.
"Hooray! The dolphins, at last!" said Sister.

Soon the show began. The dolphins jumped and leaped and spun. The trainer told them to do tricks. The Bears clapped and clapped.

18

A whale leaped out of the water. The trainer fed him fish. The Bears clapped and clapped and clapped. What a show!

As the show came to an end, the trainer asked Brother and Sister to help. Sister told a dolphin to leap. Brother fed a fish to the whale.

The whale and the dolphin made a big splash. The family got all wet!

"SPLASH!" yelled Honey. They laughed and laughed and laughed.

The Berenstain Bears
Come Clean
for School

It was the first day back to school in Bear Country.
Brother and Sister Bear were up bright and early.
After washing up, they hurried downstairs to join
Mama, Papa, and Honey Bear for breakfast. Papa
was coming to school, too, as a parent helper.

Mama had bowls of hot oatmeal ready with "Have a Great Day!" written in raisins.

"Thanks, Mama!" said Sister, digging into her oatmeal.

"Oh boy! I love raisins on my—*ah-ahh-ahhh-CHOO!*—oatmeal," Papa said, as he sneezed.

"Bless you!" said Mama. "But you should really cover your mouth and nose when you sneeze, Papa, so you won't spread germs."

"Germs?" said Papa. "Who's worried about a few germs among friends?"

Before Mama could say anything about Papa's views on germs, the cubs were heading out the door with Papa.

"Have a nice first day of school," said Mama. "Oh wait—you should wash your hands. That's another way to keep germs from spreading."

"Wash our hands?" said Papa. "They look clean enough to me. Come along, cubs."

Mama sighed. It was hard to get the family to follow good health rules. *I do hope they learn more about them in school*, Mama thought.

At the bus stop, some cubs were coughing and sneezing. Most didn't bother to cover their mouths and noses. Sister gave her best friend, Lizzy Bruin, a big hug.

"Hiya, Lizzy!" said Sister. "Are you ready for school?"

"I doan feel berry good," said Lizzy, with a stuffy nose. "I thing I'm coming down wid a coad."

"Poor Lizzy!" said Sister. "You sound awful."

Papa shook hands with Lizzy's dad, who was also a parent helper for the day. But Mr. Bruin had a cold and kept blowing his nose. He sounded like a foghorn.

Soon the bus pulled up and they all climbed aboard.

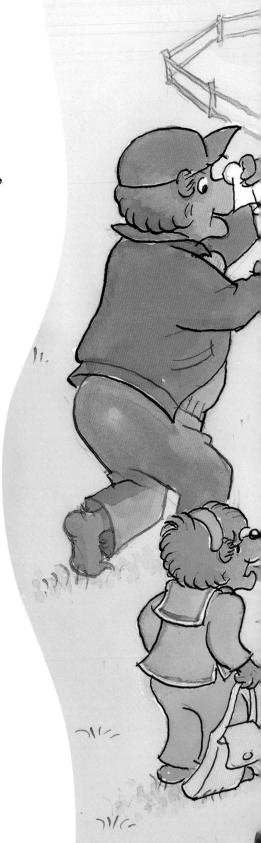

When they got to school, they found there was going to be a special assembly. Dr. Gert Grizzly was giving a talk about good health rules. Inside the auditorium, the school custodian, Grizzly Gus, was setting up a slide projector with Mr. Bruin.

"Hiya, Gus!" said Papa, shaking hands.

Grizzly Gus had a bad cough, but he didn't bother covering his mouth while he worked. Mr. Bruin kept blowing his nose.

The two of them made quite a racket. "Cough! Cough! *HONK!*"

Principal Honeycomb introduced Dr. Grizzly, and the slide show began.

"Hello, cubs!" she said. "Today I want to tell you about something that's important for good health— coming clean!"

"Now let's talk about germs! They're too small to see except close-up through a microscope, like this. Germs are everywhere. Most of them don't hurt you. But some of these little guys are big trouble.

"This is the common cold germ. It's very, very tiny, but it can make you very, very sick. Some of you are coughing and sneezing. This little character is causing all the trouble.

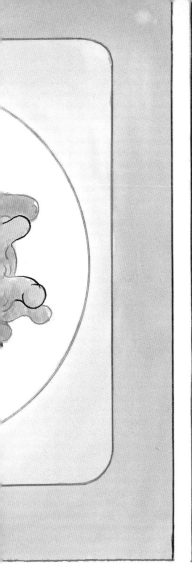

"What can we do about germs?" Dr. Grizzly asked the crowd. "We can start by making sure we don't spread them around. When we cough or sneeze, lots of germs get into the air. Then someone else may breathe them in and get sick. Always sneeze into your elbow and cover your mouth when you cough. That keeps germs from spreading.

"But the biggest germ spreaders are hands. Germs get on our hands, and we spread them by shaking hands or putting things in our mouths.

"To stop this, all you have to do is wash your hands. Washing with soap and hot water gets rid of germs. Always wash your hands before you eat and after you use the bathroom. In fact, it's a good idea to wash your hands whenever they are dirty. Try to wash for as long as it takes to sing 'Happy Birthday to You' twice.

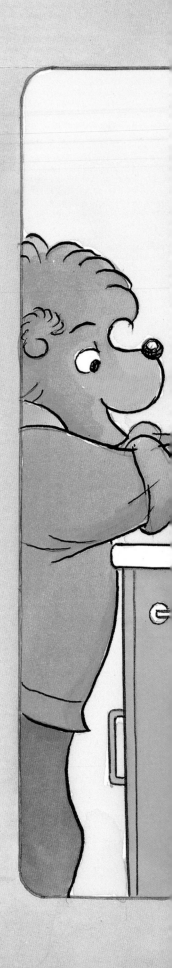

"Now here's a friend of mine, Jerry the Germ, with a special message."

The cubs all laughed and clapped and the slide show was over.

"Now," said Principal Honeycomb, "I want to see all of you get off to a good start by going back to class and washing your hands."

Ah-ahh-ahhh-CHOO!

HELPER

The cubs were soon getting lathered up in the class art sink.

"Aren't you going to wash your hands, Papa?" asked Sister.

"Oh, piffle!" said Papa. "My hands are clean enough. I don't see what the big fuss is over a few little—*ah-ahh-ahhh-CHOO!*—germs."

"Bless you!" said Sister.

When the cubs got home from school that afternoon, they told Mama about what they had learned. Mama was very pleased.

"Isn't that wonderful!" she said. "That's just the message I've been trying to get across. What do you think, Papa?"

But Papa just sneezed. "*Ah-ahh-ahhh-CHOO!*"

"Bless you!" said Mama. "Are you all right?"

"I doan feel berry good." Papa sniffled. "I thing I'm coming down wid a coad."

So Mama and the cubs put Papa to bed and gave him some nice hot soup. Then they all went and washed their hands!

Ah-ahh-ahhh-CHOO!

The Berenstain Bears'
COMPUTER TROUBLE

It was Papa who first brought a computer home to the Bear family's tree house. He thought it would be useful in his furniture business. But Papa soon found that Brother and Sister were coming into his shop to play video games on his computer.

Before long, the cubs needed their own computers for schoolwork. Email, websites, IMing, and social networking followed.

Mama discovered buying and selling things on e-Bear and wanted a computer, too. Even Honey Bear began playing simple computer games on a toy computer. Now it seemed to Papa that the whole family spent most of their time in front of computers every day from early morning until late at night.

Finally, Papa had had enough. One afternoon, he
came in from his shop with a headache from staring at
the computer too long.

"Hello!" he called. "Is anybody home? Where is
everyone?" He headed upstairs, looking for someone to
talk to.

He came to Sister's room. To his surprise, he found Sister with her head down on her desk, crying her eyes out.

"Whatever is wrong, dear?" asked Papa, patting her back.

"It's my stupid Pawbook webpage!" Sister sobbed. "That awful Billy Grizzwold wrote on it that I'm a 'fuzzy-faced hair ball' for all my friends to see, and now they're saying we're in love!" She burst into a fresh fountain of tears.

Papa rolled his eyes. *Computers*, he thought. *Nothing but trouble!*

"Come on," he said. "Let's figure out how to deal with this on your Pawbook page."

Then Papa noticed loud music coming from Brother's room. He went next door and found Brother playing music on his computer while looking at soccer gear on a website.

"Aren't you supposed to be doing your homework?" asked Papa.

"Don't worry, Papa," said Brother, "I'm working on it between checking out websites—see?" He clicked his mouse and showed Papa his homework on the screen.

Papa rolled his eyes again as Sister called him back to her room. He peeked into Honey's room across the hall. Even she was playing a game on her computer. Farther down the hall, Papa could see Mama at her computer. She was busy bidding on something on e-Bear.

At dinner that night, Papa said, "I believe that this family is having computer trouble." Everyone looked at him in surprise.

"What sort of trouble?" asked Mama.

"We are having trouble with email, websites, Pawbook, computer games, and e-Bear," Papa said, folding his arms. "We are spending so much time

on the Internet that we don't even have time to say hello to one another these days."

Mama had been worrying about this very thing herself. She just didn't seem to be able to tear herself away from e-Bear. "Well," she said, "I guess we do need to have rules for the cubs about the Internet."

"And I'm going to turn the Internet off except for one hour each day," added Papa.

"Only one hour?" said the cubs.

"That's plenty," said Papa. "If you can't get done what you need to do on the Internet in one hour, it's not worth doing."

46

"But what will we do instead?" asked Brother.
"You can get back outside and play like you used to!" said Papa.

47

After school the next day, Brother and Sister did get outside to play like they used to. It was so much fun that they went over to Cousin Fred's and Lizzy Bruin's to get them to leave their computers and come outside, too. They all went down to the playground for some good old-fashioned exercise.

After dinner that evening, Brother and Sister went online for just one hour and were surprised to find it was plenty of time after all.

Papa learned he didn't need to waste so much time online to get his business done. Freed from the spell of e-Bear, Mama got out her old quilting kit and started work on a big quilt of birds and butterflies. She got so involved that she didn't go online for even one hour.

When the Internet hour was over, the Bear family gathered in the living room. They talked about all the things that happened that day. They talked about how Billy Grizzwold apologized for calling Sister a "fuzzy-faced hair ball." They talked about Brother's soccer practice after school and the terrific corner kick he'd bent into the goal.

Mama told them about her plans for making beautiful new quilts, and Papa told them how he had really gotten into that new batch of curly maple he had in the shop. Finally, all tired out, they got ready for bed.

The next evening, the Bear family decided that they didn't want to sit in front of a computer screen at all. They did wind up sitting in front of a screen that evening, but it was a much, much bigger one, and they got to eat popcorn, too. While Grizzly Gramps and Gran took care of Honey, they all went out to the movies.

"What will it be?" asked Papa, buying the tickets. "*Pirates of the Bearibbean*, *Beary Potter*, or *Spider-Bear*?"

"*Spider-Bear*!" they all agreed.

And *Spider-Bear* it was.

The Berenstain Bears' New Kitten

On a bright Saturday afternoon, Brother Bear was hunting bullfrogs near the Bear family tree house.

Brother hadn't had much luck, but he was about to catch a big one. Then he heard a tiny "Mew! Mew!" It was a kitten.

The kitten was trying to climb the muddy bank of the pond. It was so covered in mud that you couldn't tell what color it was.

53

Someone else was hunting bullfrogs in the same pond. "Whatcha got there?" asked Too-Tall from the bushes. Too-Tall worried Brother. He was head of the schoolyard gang.

"Never mind what I've got," said Brother, trying to hide the little kitten.

"Hey!" said Too-Tall. "A kitten! A poor little shivering kitten."

How about that? thought Brother. *Even Too-Tall has a soft spot in his heart for kittens.*

"You'd better take it home to your mother," said Too-Tall. "Here. Take it home in this!" He took off his hat and gave it to Brother Bear.

Brother was surprised. He couldn't remember the last time Too-Tall did something nice for him.

Brother ran home as fast as he could with the kitten in Too-Tall's hat. He rushed inside the tree house and showed his family the furry surprise.

"Hmm," said Mama Bear. "You go looking for bullfrogs and bring home this little kitten."

"May we keep it, Mama?" asked Sister Bear. "May we please?"

"Never mind about that," said Mama. "This kitten needs cleaning up." She turned to Papa for help.

"Papa," she said, "we need some warm water, some cotton balls, and washrags."

Mama went to work. She washed the mud off.
She cleaned the kitten's eyes. She cleaned its paws.
Pretty soon it began to look like a kitten, not a
muddy ball of fur.

Little Lady, the family dog, came sniffing around. Little Lady barked, whined, and pawed at the table. She wanted to see what all the fuss was about.

"Papa," said Mama, picking up the dog, "would you please take Little Lady?"

"Yes, my dear," said Papa. "But first, I think the kitten needs a name."

He took a quick look at the kitten's bottom. "She's a she," he said. "So I guess we'd better give her a girl's name."

That made the cubs' ears perk up. You don't name a kitten if you're not going to keep her. They both got excited about having a new pet around the house.

"Well," said Sister, "she's gray."

Now that she was clean and dried and combed, she was a beautiful gray.

Gray, thought Sister.

"Let's name her Gracie!"

"Fine with
me," said Mama. "Now,
about keeping her. Have you
forgotten that we have a dog? Though
Gracie's a kitten now, she'll soon be a cat.
Dogs and cats don't always get along."
"Your mama's right," said Papa. "Let's
introduce them right now and find out."

61

Little Lady was underfoot again, sniffing around. Papa picked her up. He held her close to Gracie. Little Lady snarled.

Uh-oh, thought Brother, *they're not going to get along*.

Little Lady bared her teeth. But Gracie was not frightened. She reached out and popped Little Lady on the nose with her tiny sharp claws. Little Lady ran away.

"Hmm," said Papa. "I think they're going to get along fine."

"What about Gracie and Goldie, our goldfish?"
asked Brother.

"I wouldn't worry," said Papa. "Little Lady
loves Goldie. She'll protect her."

Gracie was now all clean, dry, and combed. Her fur was soft and fluffy. She was very beautiful.

"So I guess we've got a new kitten," said Mama.

"Yippee!" cried Brother and Sister.

Later that day, the Bear family took Gracie to
the vet to be checked. Little Lady went with them.
Her tail was between her legs. She looked unhappy.

The vet checked Gracie from head to toe.
"She's fine, a healthy kitten," said the vet. "But I
do have a prescription for Little Lady."

He wrote something on a piece of paper. It
read: Prescription—Little Lady might be jealous at
first. So give her at least twenty extra hugs a day.

The whole family gathered around Little Lady. Sister Bear and Brother Bear lifted her into their arms. Right then and there Little Lady got her first big hug of the day.

"Mew! Mew!" said Gracie.

The Berenstain Bears
Go Out to Eat

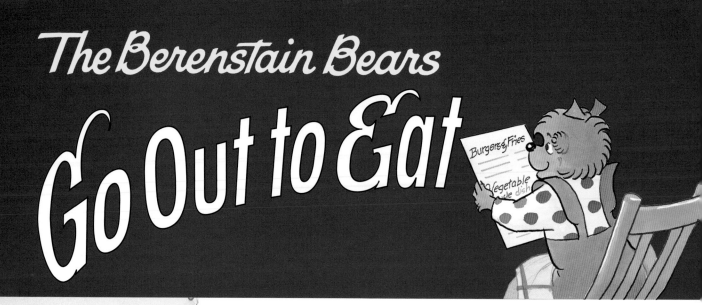

$\mathscr{E}$veryone in the Bear family works hard, but Mama Bear works the hardest of all. Of course, Papa and the cubs help with the housework as much as they can. But Mama still does most of the cleaning, cooking, washing, and ironing. On top of that, she does a lot of the gardening and yard work. Taking care of Honey Bear is almost a full-time job in itself.

Sometimes Papa and the cubs felt they all needed a break at the end of the week. One evening when Mama was tired after a long, hard day, Brother and Sister whispered something into Papa's ear.

"Hmm!" said Papa, smiling. "A very good idea."

"My dear," he said, turning to Mama, "we are all going out to eat at the Bear Country Grill. It's time you had a night off."

"Yay!" cried Brother and Sister and Honey.

It was Friday evening and everyone in Bear Country seemed to be out and about. When the family arrived at the restaurant, a crowd of customers was waiting to get in.

Papa dropped off Mama outside the restaurant while he looked for a parking spot. The lot was almost full, and Papa had to drive around and around before he found a spot right at the back of the restaurant.

"There will be a wait of about half an hour," Mama said, when Papa and the cubs joined her.

"A whole half an hour!" said Sister.

"That's nearly forever," complained Brother. "I'm so hungry!"

"I know what," said Papa. "Mama, why don't you stay here while I take the cubs for a walk?" Papa didn't really want to stand around waiting himself.

"A fine idea," agreed Mama, who thought relaxing on a bench for a while sounded quite nice.

Papa and the cubs set off toward a little duck pond on the far side of the parking lot. They saw a mother duck with ducklings. Papa had some crackers in his pocket and the cubs had a fine time feeding the ducks.

When the crackers were gone, they said good-bye to the ducks and headed back to the restaurant. By then, Mama was so relaxed she was nearly asleep.

Just then, the restaurant hostess told them that their table was ready. She led the family to their seats.

"We're starving!" said Brother and Sister, grabbing some bread.

"Just a minute," said Mama. "I don't want you two filling up on bread."

"Aw, Mama!" said the cubs.

"No arguments, please!" said Mama. "This is my evening out, and what I say goes." Mama cut each cub a slice of bread and then had the basket taken away.

"Yes, Mama," said the cubs.

Honey had a sippy cup of juice, but she wanted a big glass of water like everyone else. She leaned out of her high chair to grab one but knocked the glass over instead. Water spilled everywhere.

"Oh, dear!" said Mama, trying to sop up the water with her napkin.

"You take it easy, Mama," said Papa, leaping up. "I'll get it!" But Papa's elbow knocked over his own water, too. With some help from their server, they managed to get it all cleaned up.

"Are you ready to order now?" their server asked.

As a matter of fact, they had been too busy to look at their menus. But now they were too hungry to wait any longer.

"I'll have a hamburger and french fries," said Brother.

"Me too," said Sister.

"Just a minute," said Mama. "The hamburger is okay, but not the fries. You both need some healthy vegetables. Two side orders of broccoli, please."

"Broccoli?!" said the cubs in disappointment.

"Remember," warned Mama, "this is my evening out."

Mama and Papa ordered their dinners along with something for Honey. They had to wait and wait and wait. Mama brought coloring books and crayons out

of her bag. The cubs colored away happily for a time. But the restaurant was very busy, and they still had a long time to wait.

But just then their server arrived with a big tray full of steaming food. The whole family dug in hungrily.

"Manners, please!" said Mama. "Let's slow down a little."

Before long, almost everything was gone—except for the broccoli.

"I want to see every bit of that delicious broccoli eaten," said Mama. "It's chock-full of vitamins."

"Why do vitamins have to taste bad?" Brother grumbled, swallowing his broccoli with a gulp.

"If you eat your broccoli, you get dessert," said Papa.

"Hooray for dessert!" said the cubs.

Once the dinner plates were cleared away, everyone ordered vanilla ice cream with fresh blackberries.

"This makes up for the broccoli," said Brother.

"That's for sure!" agreed Sister.

"Sure!" said Honey.

After they finished eating, Papa paid the bill and they headed back out to their car.

"I enjoyed going out to eat," said Mama as they put Honey in her car seat. "It was just what I needed after a long, hard day!"

"Do you know what the best part of going out to eat is?" asked Brother.

"Dessert?" guessed Sister.

"Hamburger?" suggested Papa.

"No," said Brother. "It's no dishes to clean afterwards."

"That's for sure!" they all agreed as they pulled out onto the highway and headed for home.

"Sure!" said Honey.

The Berenstain Bears' DINOSAUR DIG

Brother and Sister Bear liked to read, and they went to the Bear Country Library quite often.

They liked mysteries, adventures, sports stories, and lots of other books, too.

One day, Brother found a book about dinosaurs. He showed it to Sister, and they looked at it together. It was very interesting.

Brother and Sister really liked all those dinosaurs.
Learning about them was exciting. They liked their long,
ferocious teeth. They liked their long, ferocious names—like
Stegosaurus, Triceratops, and Tyrannosaurus.

Steg-o-SAW-rus

Try-SER-o-tops

Stegosaurus had spikes on its tail. It could use them to whack big meat-eaters like Tyrannosaurus and Allosaurus, who had those ferocious teeth. Triceratops had sharp horns on its head. It could use them to poke any other dinosaurs who messed with it.

The best part was that they lived long, long ago, so you didn't have to worry about them getting you.

Tie-ran-o-SAW-rus

Mama and Papa were delighted that Brother and Sister had this wonderful new interest—and Honey thought it was okay, too. They all went to the Bearsonian Museum to see the dinosaur skeletons. They were ginormous! Brother and Sister really liked those dinosaur skeletons.

While they were at the museum, Professor Actual Factual saw them and stopped to say hello. He was the head of the museum and an old friend of the Bear family.

"I see you two cubs have been bitten by the dinosaur bug," he said, smiling.

"The dinosaur bug?" said Brother.

"What kind of bug is that?" asked Sister. She imagined a huge, prehistoric insect.

Professor Actual Factual laughed. "I just mean that you've caught an interest in dinosaurs and other prehistoric creatures. Once you've caught that bug, it's hard to get rid of it. I know—I've got it, too!

"In fact," said the professor, "would you like to see my latest dinosaur project?"

"Would we ever!" said Sister.

"You bet!" said Brother.

"Then just follow me," said the professor, leading them outside and to the rear of the museum.

They came to a big open pit in the ground. Mounds of earth were heaped up everywhere. Down in the pit, scientists were at work carefully digging away.

"What's all this?" said Papa, scratching his head.

"This is my latest dinosaur dig," explained the professor. "We have discovered a large group of dinosaur fossils right here behind the museum. We're digging them up so we can study them."

"Wow!" said Brother. "Did you find a Tyrannosaurus?"

"Well, no," said the professor. "But we did find a Spinosaurus skeleton. Spinosaurus was a fierce dinosaur almost as big as Tyrannosaurus, and it had a huge fin on its back."

"Can we see it?" asked Sister.

"Of course," said the professor. "Right this way."

They all climbed down a ladder into the dinosaur dig.

"Now, here's the Spinosaurus skeleton," said the professor. "It's the first one found in this area."

"Wowie!" said Brother. "It's humongous!"

"And over here," said the professor, "there are many other fossil reptiles."

As he led them through the dig, Brother and Sister imagined all the prehistoric creatures as they would have looked when they were alive.

They saw another fin-backed reptile, the Dimetrodon; a giant, long-necked Apatosaurus; a flying reptile, a Pterodactyl; and a giant sea reptile, the Mosasaurus. It was bigger and more ferocious than any shark that ever swam in the seas.

"Thank you for the tour, professor," said Mama, as they climbed out of the dig. "That was very interesting."

"Yeah!" said Sister and Brother together. "It was awesome!"

On the way out of the museum, they stopped in the museum shop to get more books and some dinosaur models and kits.

Back home, Brother and Sister soon had every inch of their tree house covered with model dinosaurs. There were dinosaurs and reptiles fighting on the stairs, eating on the table, sleeping on the sofa, and swimming in the bathtub. There were even some dinosaurs made of clay inside the refrigerator. Brother kept them there so they wouldn't get soft and squishy.

It seemed to Papa and Mama that dinosaurs were everywhere.

Before dinner, Papa headed for his favorite easy chair with the newspaper.

"Oh, Papa . . . ," said Sister, as he started to sit.

"Yeow!" Papa yelled, jumping up.

96

"That's my setup of the Jurassic Age," Sister explained.

"Sister," said Papa, "I'm delighted that you and Brother have this wonderful new interest. But," he said as he carefully moved Sister's dinosaurs off his chair, "the Jurassic Age will just have to settle for the coffee table."

And with a sigh, he sat down to read his paper.

The Berenstain Bears
SAFE and SOUND!

One Saturday afternoon, Brother and Sister Bear took off down the driveway on their skateboards, heading for the schoolyard. "Aren't you two forgetting something?" Mama called out. She held up their safety helmets, kneepads, and elbow and wrist guards.

"Do we really need those?" asked Brother. "We're just going down to the schoolyard for a while."

"Yeah," complained Sister, "those pads and helmets are so hot and heavy."

"Better safe than sorry!" said Mama, planting the helmets firmly on their heads.

Brother and Sister knew better than to argue with Mama. They sighed, hopped back on their boards, and headed down the road at top speed to make up for lost time.

But when they arrived at the schoolyard, instead of finding it full of cubs zipping around on their skateboards, they saw a crowd gathered around a big sign.

The sign read:
NO SKATEBOARDING
ALLOWED ON WEEKENDS.
By order of Mr. Honeycomb, Principal

"Why aren't we allowed to skateboard here anymore?" said Cousin Fred.

"Mr. Honeycomb said it's too dangerous to skateboard when the teachers aren't here to watch us," said Queenie McBear, who was always in the know.

Disgusted, the cubs picked up their skateboards and headed for home. Brother groaned. "What are we going to do now?"

Just then, Too-Tall Grizzly and his gang stepped out from behind the bushes. "Why are you Goody Two-shoes moping around?" He sneered.

"They closed the schoolyard to skateboarding," explained Brother. "Now we've got nowhere to skateboard on the weekends."

"No problem!" Too-Tall grinned. "We've got a place to skateboard."

Brother and Sister brightened up. "Really?" they said. "Where?"

"Our own private skate park," said Too-Tall, putting his arm around Brother's shoulders. "Just step this way!"

Too-Tall's skate park was jammed in among the tree trunks.

"We built this ourselves," said Too-Tall. "We've got jumps and ramps, rails and half pipes."

"Wow!" said Brother. "This is great!"

"Try it out," said Too-Tall. "We've got just one rule—no safety gear allowed."

Too-Tall and the gang got on their skateboards and hit

the ramps. Brother and Sister hesitated. They could almost hear Mama saying, "Better safe than sorry!" But Too-Tall was entitled to make his own rules. It didn't take them long to drop their helmets and pads quietly in the bushes.

"WHOOPEE!" yelled Brother as he zoomed off the hollow-tree half pipe.

"GERONIMO!" shouted Sister, doing a "grab" off an old tree stump.

Then Too-Tall lost his balance on a twisty branch
rail and went flying head over heels into a sticker bush.
KER-FLUMP! The gang all took a break to dig him out.

"How many fingers can you see?" asked Brother,
holding up three fingers.

"Uh . . . twelve?" guessed Too-Tall, his eyes rolling
around.

"Maybe you should take a break, Too-Tall," said Sister.

"Nah!" He laughed. "I'm fine! Come on, you guys,
back to the ramps!"

Brother and Sister watched Too-Tall trying to get
on his skateboard. He wasn't having much success.

"Hmm!" they both said. Maybe it was better to be
safe than sorry after all.

Brother and Sister picked up their safety gear and sneaked out of the woods while Too-Tall and the gang were bouncing off the trees.

When they got home, they were down in the dumps. "What's wrong?" Papa asked. "Why are you back so soon?"

Brother explained about the schoolyard being closed to skateboarding.

"So where are you going to skateboard now?" asked Papa.

"No place," said Brother. "Too-Tall has a skate park in the woods. But he won't let us wear our safety gear and, well, we don't think that's such a good idea."

"Smart thinking," Papa said. "Now, I think I know how to solve this problem."

He went into his workshop and brought out some sheets of plywood. "We are going to build our very own skate park!" said Papa, grabbing his tools.

"YAY!" cried Sister and Brother.

Papa asked Farmer Ben if they could build the skate park in his unused back pasture. Farmer Ben thought it was a fine idea.

The Bear family all set to work. Brother and Sister were the designers, Papa was the carpenter, and Mama and Honey were the painters.

Word of the Bear family's skate park project got around the neighborhood, and before long, other bears showed up to help out.

When the park was finished, it was decided that it would be the official Bear Country Skate Park. Mayor Honeypot himself came to the opening and gave a speech. He was almost knocked over by the rush of cubs trying to get in. Even Too-Tall and his gang showed up.

But the Bear Country Skate Park had just one rule: "Safety gear must be worn at all times"—even by Too-Tall Grizzly!

"Like I always say," Too-Tall said,
"better safe than sorry!"

The Berenstain Bears' SLEEPOVER

At the end of a busy week, Sister and Brother Bear were having a Saturday night sleepover. Lizzy and Barry Bruin were Sister's and Brother's best friends. They were going to spend the night.

Lizzy and Barry's parents brought them to the Bears' tree house.

114

"I hope Lizzy and Barry sleep well tonight," said Mrs. Bruin.

"We'll make sure they don't stay up too late," said Mama Bear.

Brother and Sister showed Lizzy and Barry around the house. They helped them put their things in the bedroom. Then the family sat down for dinner. Mama made a special dinner with the cubs' favorite foods—hamburgers and french fries! Of course, there was broccoli, too! Lizzy and Barry liked it all.

After dinner, the cubs headed to the living room. They played their favorite game, Bearopoly. Lizzy was winning, and soon owned most of the tree houses. The other cubs quickly gave up. "You're too good!" they all told Lizzy.

Lizzy smiled. She was having a lot of fun.

Next, the whole family decided to watch a
movie. The cubs got to pick out their favorite
movie, *Magic Bear*. It was about the most
powerful wizard in the universe.
The wizard had a cape that
gave him magical powers!

The movie made the cubs feel very magical. They decided to put on their own magic show. They got costumes out of the attic. They ran down the stairs showing off their magical powers. The audience was Mama, Papa, and Honey.

The show went well until Barry tripped on his magic cape. He knocked over Brother, Sister, and Lizzy!

They laughed and laughed.

"The show is over!" said Mama. "Time for bed."

The cubs put on their pajamas, washed up, and brushed their teeth. But they weren't tired yet. So Mama and Papa read them a long bedtime story.

Even then, the cubs still weren't tired. "Sleepovers are fun," said Mama, "but we can't forget about the sleeping part."

The cubs knew that they shouldn't argue with Mama. They headed to bed. Papa and Mama tucked them in.

"Good night, everyone," said Mama, turning out the lights.

After putting the cubs to bed, Mama and Papa went straight to bed themselves. They were both tired from a long week of work and a long night.

But the cubs were not at all sleepy. Brother got out his flashlight. "Let's tell spooky stories!" he said.

"Yay!" said Barry. He was ready to hear something scary.

"I don't know," said Lizzy. She was already a little spooked.

Mama woke up. She thought she heard something. She woke Papa, and they went to the cubs' room. Sister and Lizzy were hiding under the covers. Brother and Barry seemed to be sleeping.

"What is going on in here?" asked Papa.

"Brother was telling a spooky story," said Sister, "and Lizzy got scared and yelled."

"That's enough spooky stories," said Mama. "Now everyone go to sleep!"

Mama and Papa went back to bed. Mama heard
something again. She woke Papa, and they went downstairs.
They found the cubs in the kitchen eating snacks.

"It is too late for snacks," Mama said.

"But Mama," said Brother, pouring a bowl of popcorn.
"We're not tired."

Sister grabbed some soda out of the refrigerator. "Yeah,"
she added, "we're having too much fun to sleep tonight."

"No arguments," said Mama. "Back to bed!" She helped
the cubs put away the snack foods and led them to their
room.

Mama and Papa went back to bed again. But Mama heard a sound in the bathroom. She woke Papa.

They found Sister and Lizzy putting on Mama's lipstick. Brother and Barry were covered in Papa's shaving cream.

"That's enough of that!" said Mama.

"But Mama," Sister cried, "don't we look fabulous?" Sister puckered up her big, red lips while Lizzy giggled.

"You can look fabulous tomorrow," said Mama. "Right now, back to bed!"

Now the cubs were worn out. They went right to sleep. Mama and Papa sat outside the cubs' room all night. They did not get much sleep.

The next morning, the cubs slept late. At eleven o'clock, Mr. and Mrs. Bruin came to pick up Lizzy and Barry.

"I was so worried about them!" said Mrs. Bruin. "I didn't sleep a wink all night!"

"Neither did we," said Papa, his eyes closing.

After Lizzy and Barry went home, Mama and Papa sat down on the sofa.

They were soon asleep.

It was Mama and Papa's turn for a sleepover!

The Berenstain Bears

AND THE BIG SPELLING BEE

Brother and Sister Bear were good students. They both liked subjects like math, science, and history. Sister was a very good speller, too.

Gwen, a classmate of Sister's, won the big school spelling bee last year. She was expected to win again. But something surprising happened one day.

First, there were class spelling bees, which led to the big school spelling bee.

"Now, everybody, stand at your seats," said Teacher Jane. "I'll give out the words and you'll try to spell them. If you get a word right, you remain standing and wait for your next turn. If you spell it wrong, you sit down."

Soon everyone in the class except Gwen and Sister was sitting down. Sister couldn't believe she was now tied with Gwen, the best speller in the class.

"Treachery," said Teacher Jane. "An act of betrayal."

"Treachery," said Gwen. "T-R-E-C-H-E-R-Y. Treachery."

"That is incorrect," said Teacher Jane. "Please sit down."

Teacher Jane turned to Sister. She was the last one standing.

"Treachery," said Teacher Jane. "An act of betrayal."

"Treachery," said Sister. "T-R-E-A-C-H-E-R-Y. Treachery."

"That is correct," said Teacher Jane. "Congratulations! You will represent our class in the school spelling bee next Tuesday in the auditorium!"

By the time Sister got home, the whole family knew she had won the spelling bee. Papa was especially excited about it.

"Congratulations, Sister!" said Papa. "If you win the spelling bee, you'll go to the big All-Schools Spelling Bee in Big Bear City!"

But Sister hadn't realized that.

"Now here's what we're going to do," said Papa.

Mama sidled over to Papa and, in a low voice, said, "Dear, could I speak to you for a moment?" She took him by the arm and led him into the dining room. "Now Papa," said Mama. "I know you're proud of Sister—I am, too—but you mustn't get carried away and put too much pressure on her."

"Me? Carried away? Ridiculous!" protested Papa. "Besides, Sister can handle the pressure! She takes after me!" Then Papa went back into the living room.

"Oh dear!" said Mama.

"Now Sister," said Papa. "Here's what we're going to do. First, I'm going up to the attic to get my old vocabulary lists from school. Then we're gonna drill, drill, drill until you're letter perfect in every word."

Papa headed up to the attic. The lists took some finding, but Papa found them.

Meanwhile, downstairs, there was a knock on the door. Sister answered it. It was Lizzy and Jill. "Can you come over and play after supper?"

"I'm afraid not, girls," said Papa, who had come down from the attic with his vocabulary lists. "Sister and I are going to be busy preparing for the school spelling bee. The way I see it, we've got a good chance of going to the All-Schools Spelling Bee in Big Bear City."

Papa was as good as his word. Every evening after school, he drilled Sister on vocabulary words.

"Destitute," said Papa. "Without money or property."

"Destitute," said Sister. "D-E-S-T-I-T-U-T-E."

"Paramount," said Papa. "The uppermost or highest."

"Paramount," said Sister. "P-A-R-A-M-O-U-N-T."

"Prehistoric," said Papa. "Of that period before recorded history."

"Prehistoric," said Sister. "P-R-E-H-I-S-T-O-R-I-C."

It was Tuesday, and the spelling bee was under way. The contestants were up on the stage. There were seven of them. The auditorium was filled with cubs and parents. Papa was there, of course. He was rooting for Sister like crazy.

Mr. Honeycomb, the school principal, was giving out the words. The words were like rockets going off and exploding into bad spelling that knocked out the contestants one by one.

It was down to two cubs: Sister and a fifth-grader.

"Vicarious," said Mr. Honeycomb. "Taking undue pleasure from the achievements of others."

"Vicarious," said the fifth-grader. "V-I-C-C-A-R-I-E-S-S, vicarious."

"That is incorrect," said Mr. Honeycomb. He turned to Sister, who was the last cub standing.

Vicarious, thought Papa out in the audience, *taking undue pleasure from the achievements of others. Good grief! That's exactly what I am doing!*

"Vicarious," said Mr. Honeycomb. "Taking undue pleasure from the achievements of others."

"Vicarious," said Sister. "V-I-C-A-R-I-O-U-S. Vicarious."

140

"Correct!" cried Mr. Honeycomb. "Which means that Sister Bear will be going to the All-Schools Spelling Bee in Big Bear City!"

Sister got a standing ovation, except from Papa, who remained seated.

"How about a little victory snack at the Burger Bear?" said Mama, as they left the school.

"Fine," said Papa.

"Sure thing," said Brother.

Sister didn't say anything. She was lost in thought.

"Er, Papa," she said, "I don't know how to say this, and I don't want to disappoint you, but I don't want to go to the All-Schools Spelling Bee in Big Bear City. I just want to go to school, play soccer, and do things with my friends."

"Disappoint me?" said Papa. "You could never disappoint me. In fact, I'm very proud of you for having the courage to stand up for yourself. Tell you what: why don't you just take off and play with your friends?"

And that's what she did.

The Berenstain Bears
ALL ABOARD!

On a bright, sunny morning, the Bear family was going on a long trip. They had planned this trip for weeks, and it was finally here.

They were going to visit their aunt Tillie, who lived many miles away. To get there, they needed to catch a train.

Brother and Sister looked down the track. Here came the train!

"WOO-HOO!" went the whistle.

The train came into the station. It was pulled by a big, shiny engine. Clouds of smoke puffed out of the smokestack. It made a lot of noise! Brother, Sister, and Honey Bear covered their ears.

The train pulled into the station and came
to a squeaky stop. Brother, Sister, and the
whole Bear family looked up at the engine car.
Someone waved from the front seat of the train.
It was Grizzly Jones, the engineer. He would be
driving the train today.

Another bear stood near the passenger car in a bright blue uniform. His name was Mr. Mack, and he was the train's conductor. He made sure the train left on time. "All aboard!" he called. The Bear family stepped inside. They didn't want to be late!

Inside the passenger car, the family quickly found their seats. Mr. Mack came along and took their tickets. He asked if they were comfortable. "If you need anything," said Mr. Mack, "just let me know."

"Thank you!" said Brother and Sister.

With that, the train suddenly jerked forward. Honey Bear thought that was funny.

The Bear family was off on their first train trip.

At first, the train started out slow, and then it moved faster and faster. The Bear family watched out the windows at the passing sites. They passed their tree house, and then they passed Ben's farm. Farmer Ben waved from his tractor.

They passed the Bear Country School where handy bear Gus was fixing the roof. They went all the way through Grizzlyville. They saw cars and streetlights. They saw stores and traffic cops.

Then the train crossed a large bridge. They saw bears in boats fishing and bears working on the railroad.

Then the train passed through a tunnel. It climbed into the mountains, past bears skiing and climbing. The train went down into the valley. The Bear family saw mountain goats and deer.

After a while, the cubs grew tired of looking out the window. Mr. Mack stopped by to check on them. He asked if they wanted to visit the engine.

Grizzly Jones was driving the train. His helper threw coal on the fire to make the train go. The cubs watched as the fire grew brighter and brighter with each shovel of coal.

Brother wanted to throw coal on the fire, too. Grizzly Jones smiled. "Maybe when you're a little older," he said with a laugh.

"But," added Grizzly Jones, "I have something you both can do for me."

"Yay!" shouted the bears with excitement.

Grizzly Jones pointed to a cable hanging above them. "Want to blow the whistle?" he asked. Brother quickly gave the cable a strong tug.

"WOO-HOO!" went the whistle.

"Now, would you like to drive the train?" asked Grizzly Jones.

Would they ever!

The cubs took turns in the driver's seat. They couldn't believe they were actually driving a train. Their friends would never believe this story!

Just then, a freight train passed them on another track. At the end of the freight train was a red caboose. It was like a little house on wheels. The train's conductor lived there. He waved as they went past.

A little while later, the cubs headed back to their seats. They were getting hungry. Mama had a lunch basket. The Bears ate as the train rolled on. Brother and Sister told Mama and Papa all about driving the train.

"You did a great job!" said Mama.

"Yes," added Papa, "the ride was very smooth."

Soon, the Bear family heard a loud squeak, and the train started to slow down. They pulled into a station. The train stopped and gave off a big puff of steam.

"Whoosh!"

"Good-bye, Mr. Mack and Grizzly Jones," said the cubs. "Thanks for the ride!"

"Thank you for the ride," said Grizzly Jones with a smile and a wink.

The Bear family all let out a laugh.

158

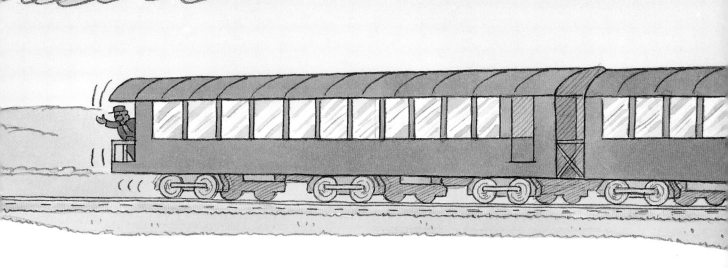

Nearby, Aunt Tillie was waiting in her car. "I want to be an engineer when I grow up," Sister told her.

"What about you, Brother?" asked Aunt Tillie.

"I want to live in the red caboose!" he said.

"So do I," said Aunt Tillie.

The Berenstain Bears
HUG and MAKE UP

The Bear family got along nicely most of the time. But even happy families who love each other very much don't get along all the time. It didn't happen very often, but there were days when the whole family got up on the wrong side of the bed.

When it happened, though, it made for a bad day in the tree house.

It could start with Brother or Sister taking too long in the bathroom on a busy school morning. It could start with somebody leaving the cap off the toothpaste tube.

It could start with somebody accidentally stubbing a toe. Yes, even Mama sometimes started off on the wrong foot. It didn't help when baby Honey decided to join in and started crying at the top of her lungs.

Things got even worse at breakfast.
Manners were forgotten. Nobody said "please
pass the jam" or "may I have the honey?"
The Bears just reached and grabbed. Their
dog, Little Lady, got a little worried and hid
under the stairs. Goldie, the goldfish, hid in
her underwater castle.

Brother finished first and shouted at Sister, who was having a second helping of cereal, "Come on, you slowpoke, or you'll make us late for the school bus!"

"Who are you calling a slowpoke, you dumbhead!" Sister shouted back. "You were the one who made us late yesterday when you forgot to have Mama sign your test paper!"

"That'll be quite enough shouting and name-calling!" roared Papa, banging the table so hard the whole tree house shook.

"And quite enough table-banging!" said Mama. "You're worse than the cubs!"

"Grrr!" said Papa, jamming his hat on his head and storming out the door.

Brother and Sister usually sat next to each other on the school bus. But this morning they came onto the bus looking like storm clouds.

"I saved your seats for you," said their friend Lizzy Bruin.

"I wouldn't sit next to him if he were the last bear on earth!" said Sister.

"That goes double for me!" said Brother, stomping to the rear of the bus.

And all through recess and lunch break they refused to have anything to do with each other.

As soon as they got home from school, the shouting and arguing started all over again. They argued about where to have their after-school milk and cookies: at the kitchen table or in front of the television.

They argued about which video to watch: *The Bear Stooges* or *The Bearbie Show*. Soon they were rolling around on the floor, fighting over the remote.

"I've had quite enough of this fussing and feuding! There'll be no television today!" said Mama. She not only took away the remote, she pulled the plug on the television. "Just sit yourselves down and do your homework, and I don't want to hear another peep out of either of you!"

Brother and Sister sat at the dining-room table and tried to do their homework. But they were so busy looking daggers at each other that they couldn't concentrate.

By the time Papa came in from his shop, the Bears' bad day had become a full-fledged family feud. Little Lady was still hiding under the stairs, and Goldie was still hiding in her castle. Angry silence filled the air.

Grim-faced Brother was trying to reach the next level on one of his video games, but he kept falling short. Tight-lipped Sister was coloring in a coloring book, but she wasn't staying in the lines very well.

Angry Mama
was trying to read
a magazine. So Papa
sat down glowering
and pretended to read the
newspaper. But it's hard for
folks who love each other to stay angry all day, especially
if they really don't have anything to be angry about.

"Mama," Sister said.

"Yes?" said Mama.

"That magazine you're
reading," said Sister, starting
to giggle. "You've got it
upside down!"

"Why, so I do," said
Mama with a small
giggle of her own.

Now, it happens that giggling is as contagious as the twenty-four-hour virus.

More quickly than it takes to tell, the whole Bear family was laughing uproariously. (Except for baby Honey, who until that moment was having a long nap.)

They were laughing so hard their sides hurt. They laughed so hard tears rolled down their cheeks.

And what were they laughing at? They were laughing at themselves for wasting a whole day being angry about nothing.

Little Lady came out from under the stairs, Goldie came out of her underwater castle, and Honey Bear saw her once angry family dry their tears and hug and make up.

The Berenstain Bears' Really BIG PET SHOW

The Bear family loved their pets, and they took good care of them. They took their dog, Little Lady, for walks every day.

They played with their cat, Gracie, with a ball of string or a toy mouse. They kept the bowl of their goldfish, Goldie, sparkling clean.

One morning, the family went down to the Bear Country Pet Store to shop for their pets. Brother, Sister, and Honey Bear loved visiting the store. Brother liked to watch the puppies. Sister liked to pet the kittens.

Honey Bear liked the birds best of all. "Tweet!"
said Honey Bear to a cage full of canaries.

"Tweet! Tweet! Tweet!" sang the canaries.

"Chirp!" said Honey Bear to a cage full of finches.

"Chirp! Chirp! Chirp!" chirped the finches.

Then Honey Bear saw a cage of parakeets. "Bird!"
she said, pointing to them.

A bright blue parakeet cocked its head. "Bird!" it
said, as plain as could be. "Bird! Bird! Bird!"

"That bird can talk!" said Sister.

"It's a parakeet," explained Papa. "Parakeets can imitate sounds and words."

"Neat!" said Brother. "Can we get a parakeet?"

"I don't know," said Mama. "We already have three pets."

Honey Bear pressed up against the bars of the birdcage. "Keets!" she said, trying to say "parakeets."

"Keets!" the parakeet said back. "Keets! Keets! Keets!"

"Keats! That would be a good name for him," Sister said, laughing.

Once they had picked out a name for the parakeet, they couldn't just leave him in the pet store. So Keats the parakeet went home to the tree house with the Bear family.

Keats was easy to take care of. They fed him birdseed every day and gave him water.

They cleaned his cage, and once a day they let him out to fly around for exercise.

"You know," said Papa one evening, looking around at all their pets, "this place is getting to be a regular pet show."

"A pet show," said Mama to herself. "Hmm!"

Mama was the Chair of the Beartown Festival Committee. The Beartown Festival was a big street fair that was held every year in Beartown Square. The committee was looking for something to do at the festival that would be fun for the cubs. A pet show seemed like a pretty good idea.

A few days later, Mama came home from a Beartown Festival Committee meeting. "It's all settled," she told the family. "There's going to be a big pet show at the Beartown Festival this year."

"Can we enter Little Lady, Gracie, Goldie, and Keats?" asked Brother.

"Of course!" said Mama.

"Hooray!" yelled Brother and Sister, jumping up and down.

"Ray!" yelled Honey Bear.

"Ray!" imitated Keats. "Ray! Ray! Ray!"

When the day of the big pet show arrived, the Bear family and their pets all piled into the car to drive to Beartown Square. It was quite a scene. There were cubs with their pets from all over Bear Country.

Some cubs had truly unusual pets. Too-Tall Grizzly brought his pet garter snake, Slither. Barry Bruin even had a pet skunk!

"Don't worry," he told everyone. "He's deodorized!"

"That's a relief!" said Mayor Honeypot, who was the judge of the show.

Mayor Honeypot had a clipboard, and he took notes about all the pets. Brother and Sister wondered if their pets had a chance to win a prize ribbon.

The mayor came to Keats's cage. "What's your name, little bird?" said the mayor. "My name is Mayor Honeypot."

"Honey!" said Keats. "Honey! Honey! Honey!"

The mayor laughed. "What a clever little bird!" he said, and made a note on his clipboard.

Finally, Mayor Honeypot climbed up on a platform to announce the winners. "After much careful thought," he began, "I have decided that I can't decide. Since all the pets here are very, very special, I believe that they all should receive a ribbon!"

"YEA!" cried all the cubs.

There were ribbons for the biggest pet and the smallest pet . . . for the fanciest cat and the cutest cat . . . for the shaggiest dog and the scratchiest dog.

Barry Bruin's skunk got a ribbon for "Most Unusual Pet" and Too-Tall Grizzly's snake for "Quietest Pet."

Little Lady got the ribbon for "Best Collar" and Gracie for "Biggest Bow." Goldie was "Best Behaved." And Keats was given the ribbon for "Cleverest Bird."

"We always thought Keats was clever," Sister told Mayor Honeypot when he pinned the ribbon on the parakeet's cage. "Now we have a ribbon to prove that he is the cleverest bird in Bear Country!"

"One small correction," said the mayor, looking inside the cage. "*She* is the cleverest bird in all Bear Country!"

They looked inside the cage. There, resting on the bottom, was a little white egg.

"Where did that come from?" asked Sister.

"I guess Keats must have laid it," said Papa, scratching his head.

"Then Keats . . . is a girl!" Brother said. "But 'Keats' doesn't sound like a girl's name. Maybe we should change it to 'Keatsie.'"

"How about 'Cutsie'?" suggested Sister.

"Perfect," agreed Brother. "Our clever little parakeet, Cutsie!"

"Cutsie," said Honey Bear.
"Cutsie! Cutsie! Cutsie!"
repeated the Cleverest Bird.